MW00466121

Breakfast at the Good Hope Home

To Sis Recke,
Enjoy,
Mike Bayles

Mike Bayles

918studio press
Davenport, Iowa

Copyright © 2017 Mike Bayles

All rights reserved. No part of this book may be used or
reproduced by any means, graphic, electronic, or
mechanical, including photocopying, recording, taping or
by any information storage retrieval system without the
written permission of the publisher except in the case of
brief quotations embodied in critical articles and reviews.

Breakfast at the Good Hope Home is a fictional/poetic
account of a son's experience visiting his father with
Alzheimer's disease in a nursing home. It reflects the
state of understanding of the disease between 1885 and
the early 1990's. All of the characters, names, incidents,
organizations, and dialogue in this novel are either the
products of the author's imagination or are used
fictionally.

ISBN: 978-0-9851944-9-9
Library of Congress Control Number: 2016918728

ACKNOWLEDGMENTS

I would like to thank Jodie Toohey for her careful editing. Erin Bertram also provided thoughtful comments and encouragement. Writers' Studio and members Steve Lackey, Phyllis Kinney, and Mary Davidsaver critiqued my manuscript. The Midwest Writing Center has been a valuable resource for me. I would also like to thank the website for The Alzheimer's Association and Web MD. Thank you to Renee Busha and Sliced Moon Designs for the cover art and design.

The poem, "Old Botany," appearing on page 27, is a poem published in the poetry collection, *Threshold*, by Mike Bayles.

Fred, my dad, thinks he is still in the house. He gets out of his chair and shuffles across the floor. I watch. I wonder if I have to tell him to eat.

Last night I barely slept after the court and his conservator placed him in the Good Hope Home. What had been a matter of managing family finances had become a matter of my father's state of mind after the conservator had said that my father didn't seem to understand. Now the house I knew and his life were falling apart, as was mine.

The mattress and the weight of decisions made pressed upon me around the time of the hearing. Just as when I was a child, my dark room was the loneliest place to be when I couldn't sleep.

Still living in the house with my mom, I visit him alone.

Someone brings a tray of food, and he stares at it.

"Aren't you going to eat?" I ask, as if he's a child. "Have a bite for me."

I ask myself what I am doing there. The *how's* and *why's are* difficult to comprehend. A crucifix hangs on the wall.

After spending years learning to be his son, I now must learn to be his father.

Someone in the hallway moans, as if in Hades. I close the door, figuring Dad doesn't need to hear. I wonder if he's going to become like the man in the hallway.

I grab a fold of the red sweatshirt I had given him. Gold letters on the front say *IOWA STATE UNIVERSITY*, the place where he had sent me to get my Bachelor's Degree in Sociology. I take a napkin from the tray and wipe oatmeal off his chin.

After he stops eating, he sits up in the bed and looks at me. "What did I do?" he asks. Tears fill his eyes.

I want to explain, but can't. It's not exactly what he has done, and it's not who he is, but it's what he has become. I close my eyes for a moment to envision an image of him during summer days spent at our summer cottage on a lake.

Leaves on the tree outside the window are brown.

I turn to him and say, "Alzheimer's," while doubting the word.

He spews out some garbled words and points at a red footrest.

"That's a nice footrest," I say.

He utters some word that sounds like *lathe*. I nod and laugh, realizing he is trying to sell me a machine tool. "You told me that you'd never retire."

Three years ago, he was a sales engineer, working for his own machine tool sales company.

Someone taps at the door, and a CNA wearing a maroon uniform comes into the room. Freckled and with dark, red hair, she looks as if she's just graduated from college. Her name tag says, *Becky*.

I feel the warmth of her smile as she greets me. She turns to Dad and says, "You sure haven't eaten a lot."

He puckers his lips, and she steps back from the bed.

"At least, he knows how to do that," I say.

I look at the clock on the wall and think about the appointment for work I had cancelled. "I hope that my supervisor understands the time I've taken off from work."

Becky nods.

MENU FOR AUGUST 23RD

ONE CUP OF OATMEAL
ONE CARTON OF ORANGE JUICE

SERVE WITH A SMILE

Logic hurts confused minds,
and how's and why's become useless
when what matters
is the sound of your voice.

Play along with things
you don't understand,
but don't aggravate
and don't ask too much.

Seek safe topics
ignore right or wrong
and touch upon memories
to find common ground.

Go ahead.

He's your father.

The only way
to detect Alzheimer's disease
is to dissect his brain
like Medieval wizards
looking for soul
only to kill another victim
the essence of life a mystery
all left to the gods.

Your father's passed his physicals
and lacks any apparent cause.
It is our conclusion
that he has this disease of brain.
His body is healthy,
but we know he will die.

Alzheimer's disease is a type of dementia that causes problems with memory. Symptoms usually develop slowly and get worse over time, becoming severe enough to interfere with daily tasks.

My supervisor at Child Welfare Services leads me into a meeting room after I ask about my schedule for the next week. She tells me to grab a sugar cookie on her desk first.

Two social workers walk past the door as she opens a case folder. She mentions the most recent court review. "You will continue bringing the children to the home for supervised visits. The father will continue going to therapy, and the mother will take a course on parenting."

I thumb through the plan and nod.

I look at the bags under her eyes and wonder if she's as tired as me. She has been working on the annual report at night, as well as helping her brother, who moved in with her husband and the family.

She asks me, "And how are you doing?"

"Fine, I guess. Why are you asking?"

"We're all a little concerned. How was your day off?"

"Fine, except for the court hearing." I shake my head. "I sent Dad to the nursing home on my birthday."

"It must have been really hard for you."

I look up at the ceiling, as if looking for an answer, and sigh, "You do what you have to do."

"How's your mother taking this?"

"She kept looking at me when I was testifying, and she was smiling. After the hearing she was still smiling. I don't think she understood."

"Did she say anything?"

"After the hearing she kept telling the lawyers she could take care of him. He looked back at her and said that Dad will be better off in a home. She kept looking as he and another lawyer led him off to a car."

"Do you believe she can?"

"He wandered off one day and got lost."

My supervisor excused herself and got me a cup of water. "Don't worry; we've got someone to cover the visit for you today."

"It was so hard. I had to work with the kids and their parents, and then go home to watch Dad, and he didn't listen to me."

"That's what parents say about their kids."

"I know."

I say I'm family,
and a nurse buzzes me
into the ward
locked for their protection.
Patients wandering through hallways groan,
and I wonder about the worlds
they inhabit and languages
without words.
They pass each other
without acknowledgement,
to the smell of bleach and poop.

The family home is broken and silent, and I don't know which is worse.

Salmon tiles from the shower are missing, although Dad replaced them. A burner on the stove doesn't work. Dad blamed me when it sparked.

A short in the air conditioner left the house unbearably hot.

Mom watches while I pick up the last box to take to my just-rented room in a boarding house. "I can't stay anymore," I say.

We haven't been able to talk for the last three days.

Dad once said that he was worried when she told him that she saw flying saucers.

I look to the ceiling and tell him I'll keep an eye on her. I listen for him, but only hear echoes in my mind.

Mom stands outside the front door while I put the last box into my car.

Silence is worse.

The Good Hope Home opened its Alzheimer's Unit on August 1st. Mayor Eric Swanson spoke at the ribbon cutting ceremony, saying it was a good addition to the community. The Good Hope Home Director, Tom Smith, said that the home is expanding to meet community needs. This is the first Alzheimer's unit in the metro area. An open house will be held on September 14th. Cake and ice cream will be served.

Mom and I share a complicit agreement that we will visit my dad separately. We hold different beliefs about what the family is.

In her words and deeds, I'm still her little boy. By moving out, I'm saying that I'm not.

Even Dad told her to give me my own space.

She never mentions the court hearing. She's never been angry about it, and if she was, she'd never stay angry with me.

It's for his own good, I keep telling myself, although she doesn't believe.

I drive to see him on Sundays when I'm off work. A neighbor takes her in the middle of the week.

When I stop by to see her, there's little to say, except, "It's too bad" and "It's a shame."

She believes he's coming home.

THINGS MY DAD USED TO LIKE TO DO	THINK I LIKE TO DO OR USED TO LIKE
Running a mile all out on small town streets	Running ten miles on a bike path
Watching me run 10K races	Running 10K races
Having hot fudge sundaes	Having chocolate sundaes
Working day and night	Working day, playing night
Working two machine tools in a factory at the same time for small raise	Taking new position at Child Welfare for the same pay
Working late night on specifications to sell machine tools	Working early nights on case notes and playing with parakeet
Watching the Beatles on *The Ed Sullivan Show*	Watching the Beatles on *The Ed Sullivan Show*
Listening to "Yesterday" played on my stereo	Playing "Yesterday" on my stereo
Talking about business	Talking about war protest and social

causes

Letting me drive the car he just bought	Driving the car he just bought
Visiting me at college	Going away to college
Pulling dandelions and picking up litter	Mowing the grass on his riding mower
Going out with my mom and me	Going out on my own
Raising children	Raising parakeets
Being married	Going on dates

While standing at Dad's bedside, I say, "I miss you."

I wonder if he misses me or if he knows he misses me.

Silence is an answer and a question.

Becky, the CNA, walks into the room, and I smile at her.

"How are you doing?" she says to him, as if they are friends.

I feel alone, and want her to be my friend.

There are two deaths with Alzheimer's disease: death of the personality and death of the body. Death of the body can come years after the former.

In second grade, Sister Mary said that the soul never dies.

Your father's doing well. He still has his appetite. There's one thing, though. He gets agitated when your mother comes to visit. She keeps telling him that he's going home.

I start to apologize, but she stops me.

Your father gets agitated at night. He hits us when we try to put him to bed.

He almost hit me at home. He hit Mom when she tried to explain something.

Logic hurts.
So does a good punch.

Mom calls. She tells me that Dad has fallen and hit his head. "They'll X-ray him at the hospital, to look for brain damage," she says.

I wonder why.

I call my supervisor and tell her I'll be late. She'll have to make some calls. It will have to be later when I take the children to their parents' house and supervise the visit. I hope they will understand.

A tire goes flat on the way to Mom's. There's more to explain, and I have to find the answers.

I must give the parents two hours of time with their children, or they'll complain to the social worker.

There's a birthday party in the Community Room when we get to Good Hope. A sign says, *Ninety Years Young*, but I know Dad won't make it that long. A group of children sing. Grandchildren, I figure.

A belt keeps Dad in a chair in his room. His head is tilted backwards, and his mouth is open. He takes a deep breath as we approach. I wonder what he sees.

I glance at Mom. *Don't tell him that you're taking him home*, I think. *Please.*

Becky says, "Your father just slid off the chair while watching the TV."

I walk up to him and tease him as I always have. "I told you to wear a helmet while riding the bicycle."

Only I laugh.

In the later stage of the disease patients lose motor control.

Alzheimer's symptoms vary. The general guide below can provide a general idea of how abilities can change during the course of the disease.

Stage 1: No impairment
Stage 2: Very mild decline
Stage 3: Mild decline
Stage 4: Moderate decline
Stage 5: Moderately severe decline
Stage 6: Severe decline
Stage 7: Very severe decline

First steps and walking,
a toddler dreams,
sitting in a big boy chair
before taking strides
and learning to fly
while his father watches
with pride
school and college coursework
and a lifetime of work
as young adults learn

until the latest stages

when an adult unlearns
work of a lifetime
school and college coursework
with quiet despair
as his son watches
father falls
losing strides
now belted in an old man's chair
remnant memories
of first steps and walking

Accumulations of plaque
twist and kill cognition,
whether from aluminum cookware
we can only speculate causes
of plaque that kills the brain
in a man, who in early stages
otherwise appears healthy.
When there's something we can't cure
it hurts to say, it's in someone else's hands.

Each morning we get him up, dress him and get him in the chair. He seems to like it when he wears the red Iowa State University sweatshirt. It fits him well. Did he go there?

I did.

It fits him well as a memory, and it is helpful to give a patient things from their past. Did you give it to him?

I did.

He may not remember that you gave it to him, and on bad days, he might not even recognize you, but it's important that you visit and talk to him. Can you?

I don't know.

It's important.

I guess I can.

It seems to help.

Every day they dress him
as if he's got somewhere to go.

They pick his clothes
and put him in the sweatshirt I bought him.

Every few days they shave him
for visitors who may come.

The sweatshirt I gave
stirs memories of college days
and his visits there.

When a foot steps on a wooden floor
another chamber of Old Botany stirs.
I listen to the many ways the building
      speaks
to the many parts of me,
the room where I take Intro to Psychology,
and the hallway where samples of seedlings
in wire cages break ground as I.
Cubicles cluster around a commons area
where students offer psyches
for graduate student grades.
On second, a maze winds its way
to teaching assistant offices
where I ponder trials of life.
Stories linger about third floor,
a place some say is abandoned,
unable to bear the weight of other lives,
unseen and left to wonder.
A step outside shows the aging face
observant of a verdant Central Campus
while I shadow its incarnations.

CNAs sitting on a bench between two wards smoke. Becky flashes a smile. I take a moment and talk with them. Unlike my father, I know she will answer.

Children on bikes gather on the circular drive.

I ask her what they are doing.

"They like to ride down the hill." She laughs. "The daredevils."

"Mom would tell me not to do it, and Dad would let me do it if I wanted to."

"Did you?"

"Yeah, and I wiped out in front of my friends."

"How embarrassing."

I chuckle. "They laughed, and Dad told me to get up."

One boy goes down the hill and another shouts, "Cool."

Memories stir inside me, of a time when children always stay young and dads never die.

"It's strange kids come to a nursing home," I say.

Becky nods. "Before it was a nursing home, it was a park. Children used to come here, play games and ride a Ferris wheel. There was so much to do that they could stay all day."

When the city was young
children biked from home
to ride the Ferris wheel.
After a worker strapped them
into their gondolas
the wheel turned
round and round
up and down,
and their world
grew smaller and larger,
and each time
when the ride paused
the gondola on top swayed,
the children took in sights
of the vista spread before them,
heavenly visions offered
when the city was young.

What Dad said about his family:

My mom told me to chew everything until it is liquid.

When the first cars came to town, one of my uncles paid no attention to them. He was run over by one and killed.

My grandmother choked to death at a Thanksgiving dinner, and all I could do was watch.

I haven't talked to my older brother in years, but my younger sister still calls.

The way others taught us how to swim was to throw us into the quarry lake. It was sink or swim.

I had this uncle who liked to float on his back on a lake. Once he fell asleep. In the morning everyone found him still floating on his back.

This time Becky sits on the bench alone. She leans her back against the bench.

I sit next to her. "I haven't seen you in a few weeks."

"I've been off work."

I look at her.

"I hurt my back lifting a patient."

"It must be rough."

Her hand brushes against mine. "Your father has been moved to Building Two."

People enter and leave at will.

"Is it a locked ward?"

"No, but he won't go anywhere."

Your father has lost most of his reasoning
and recognition, and at times
he might not recognize you,
but still he needs you
for stimulation of his mind,
or something inside.
I want to remind you
that a little stimulation
might slow his decline.

Dad Working = House For Family

My Working Part Time = Me Coming Back Home

Dad's Machine Tool Sales Business Going Under
+ Unpaid Property Taxes = Worry

Mom Telling Dad that the City and County Are
Stealing the House + Talk of Conspiracy = His
Aggravation

Explanations = Dad Might Hit Me + Logic Hurts

Dad's Failure to Understand + His Troubles at
Home + My Testimony = His Placement at Nursing
Home

A Business Going Under + Unpaid Property Taxes
+ Cost of the First Year at the Nursing Home = The
House Must Be Sold

Grief Borne Separately + Misunderstandings + My
Old Wounds = I Move to an Apartment

The house is sold, and a moving company is taking Mom's belongings to an apartment a social worker rented in her name. She takes my old toys, college textbooks, and drawings with her.

She takes literature and specifications from his business, gone under.

Taxes and the first year in the nursing home must be paid. Dad said that someone stole the house. He might be right.

What can't be kept in Mom's apartment is stored in a wire cage in the basement. Memories are stored.

The house that Dad bought
when I was away at college,
now lies in darkness
of fallen night.

The master bedroom
that my parents shared
is bare.
My bedroom, now without
the stereo, silent.

I wonder if Dad still remembers
"Yesterday," the song I played
for him after coming home.

It lies in disrepair,
broken tiles and memories
on the marketplace,
wanting to be sold,
waits to be shaped
around the life of another family.

It wants to be whole,
the house that Dad bought.

He must feel as if he's falling
when CNAs put him to bed,
those robbers whom he feels
are stealing his very soul.

...

The falling sun
and dissonant dreams
lay claim to the nightmare
stirring inside the plaque
that clutters his brain.

The plaque inside his head is killing his brain cells. First the brain dies, then the body. Although he has lost weight, he still might look healthy to the casual observer.

Dad's vision shrinks
from the promised house and yard
to the one in disrepair and broken tiles
to the locked ward in the home
to the room he shares
to his own side
to the ceiling
so white
above.

We no longer need to tie your father down. He isn't going anywhere.

We used to give him tranquilizers, but not now. We're trying a kinder approach.

Remember, it's important that you see your father. Speak to his memories. Keep talking to him even if he doesn't answer. Even with all the research, we don't understand. Speak to him, it's out of our hands.

Visitors make all the difference in the world.

> A silent room is where you stay
> and look at the ceiling.
> The nickname I used to call you
> I hope resonates memories.
> *Baldy*, an old nickname, I say.
>
> You don't say anything,
> but a man in the next bed stirs,
> to a language only I understand.
>
> I hope I'm speaking to something
> somewhere inside you that understands.
> Memories and spirits call, and spirits
> cannot be dissected.
>
> Dad. Dad?

When I was a child a priest said that we couldn't know the future. It would be too much to bear. Now as an adult, I can't believe what is happening to Dad. The child inside of me cries.

Becky tells me the grounds of the nursing home used to be a mental hospital, then a park.

Friends say a mental patient is buried in the wooded ravine behind the nursing home.

Dad once said that when he was a child, he heard patients scream in a mental hospital near his hometown. He said that he was afraid of them.

He's living on the grounds where a mental hospital used to be.

Some staff say down the hill
an unmarked grave lies
containing the remains
of a former mental patient.

An unmarked grave lies
under the cover of foliage
a former mental patient-
no one knows his name.

Under the cover of foliage
someone says lies a broken man.
No one knows his name,
only conversations of what used to be.

Someone says, lies a broken man
somewhere down the hill.
Only conversations of what used to be
remain.

Becky and I sit and watch children go down the hill. Each dares another to go next, who first declines. In a cacophony of voices, they call each other *Chicken* and *Scaredycat* while crows walking across the grounds chatter.

I turn to Becky. "What can you tell me about the hospital that was here?"

"Oh, I don't know. It was called a sanatorium." She laughs. "Sometimes I think the story was made up to scare away the kids."

"I don't think the story is working."

A boy runs across the grounds, and crows scatter into the air.

"I remember when I used to play," I tell her.

"I grew up on a farm and played with my older brothers," she says.

"When do they go home?"

"It won't be long. The sun is now setting early."

"Where did the summer go?"

A red and white checkered table cloth is on the table brought from the house when I get to Mom's apartment. Three places are set, and I ask, "Are we having company?"

"Your father's coming."

I give logic a try. "How's he going to get here?"

"Don't worry, he's coming."

I shake my head. He can't even get out of bed.

She goes into the kitchen, and I go to the living room to watch a football game. Neighborhood children play in the yard, recalling times when I was young.

Mom taps me on the shoulder, and says, "Supper's ready."

I prefer to call it dinner.

"I'll look to see if he's coming," she says.

I look out the window and see no one in particular, as expected.

"He's not here."

"I'll save some for him."

The television plays, and his food is getting cold.

The maple tree, still green,
silhouetted before pale blue sky.
I once sat with my father in a park
to complete the assignment
and capture the fullness
before the leaves would fall.
Steady was my hand,
intense my desire
to show every leaf,
but instead,
I drew the tree as whole,
and with great diligence
I conveyed its grand shape.
I took note of its place in the landscape,
a part of the grand design,
and my father watched
while just downhill
the timeless river flowed.

Dad, the leaves are falling outside your window.

I wish you could see them.

trees mourn naked forms
winds brush limbs
change seasons
days of passing
warm spell recalls memories
passing of days
seasons change
limbs brush winds
forms naked mourn trees

I grab Becky's wrist after she and her supervisor step out of Dad's room. Becky turns toward me, brushing a strand of hair from her eye. She looks pale. "Are you okay?"

The supervisor steps away from her, and says, "Don't take too long, you're needed in room 104."

"How's my dad?" I ask.

"We have to diaper your father," she says.

"Diaper? But he's my dad."

Her supervisor says, "These things happen."

Becky grabs my arm and says, "I'm sorry."

She goes to room 104, and for a moment I stand alone, left with more questions.

From sleeping all the time, to crawling to walking to talking, so it is with your father in reverse. Talking ends, and walking ends, and he can't even crawl.

Only son to caretaker, intelligent father to someone helpless.

The supervisor says from child to a parent's caretaker, the adult to a child. These things happen.

These things are happening to him and me.

He stares at the ceiling
as I talk, and I ask why
and to whom, this man
who looks like my dad,
silence and empty spaces
and sunlight through window
falls upon his shrunken frame
feet barely pushing up his bed sheet,
and he's a shadow of himself.

A spirit? I wonder.
I wonder where inside my father lies
this essence to reach
when I only have
the sound of my voice to offer,
memories and caring beyond logic,
a belief I hope is true,
that I am talking to the soul.

Becky steps into the room as Dad struggles to breathe. She places a moist washcloth on his forehead. "The doctor has been called," she says. "Your father is going to the hospital."

Dad's cheeks are hollow. Now he looks old to me, and I wonder if his spirit wants escape his body.

> in death spirit free
> another life he seeks
> heavenly calling

Becky pulls me into the hallway, as if Dad can hear. "Decisions must be made," and I wonder how someone her age can understand. "Does he have a living will?"

"Not that I know." I take a deep sigh and look to the ceiling, as if looking to Heaven. "We never talked about it."

A bell rings at the nursing station, and I know we can't talk for long.

"I don't know what to do. I wish there was an easy answer," I say.

"I don't think there is."

"What do I do?"

"Talk it over with someone, maybe your mother."

"I guess I'll have to."

       decisions to make
       and time is drawing closer
       life and death calling

She steps closer and rests a hand on my shoulder. "I suppose I ought to tell you; I've been accepted to a four year nursing school."

"When?"

"In a few weeks."

I hold her hand a few seconds, unsure if I should be happy or sad.

An abstract painting of an angel hangs on the wall.

Caged finches in the community room
flutter from limb to limb in a cage
without song
innocent and young
full of life and aflutter,
and this is where I go to collect my
          thoughts,
to recall memories when I was young
when he bought my first parakeet
and taught me patience I needed then,
to move slowly, a social grace
so to not startle,
and now I need patience even more.

The next morning, I drive Mom to a diner at the edge of town. She looks surprised. Snow flurries swirl around us as we walk to my car. As she stands by the passenger door, I fasten the button of her black winter coat.

"Where did summer go?" she says.

"It's been seven years since Dad was placed in the nursing home."

I pause. "Where did time go?"

A hostess at the diner shows us to a booth near the kitchen. We are interrupted by loud conversations and waitresses carrying trays of food. I wish we had something more private.

I take Mom's coat and hang it up. *Good manners are what counts*, Dad once said.

Moments later a waitress brings two glasses of water and takes our orders. I order hash browns with cheese and an iced tea with a slice of lemon. Mom orders a cup of coffee, although I offer to buy her something more.

She asks if Mom wants cream or sugar.

Mom says, "No." She doesn't want to be too much trouble.

"I think we're going to have a nasty winter," she says.

I grab her hand to get her attention. "Dad's not doing well."

The lines on her face show years of worries she's endured.

"Mom, a nurse said that we might have important decisions to make."

"We can talk about it tomorrow."

ONE HASHBROWN WITH CHEESE
ONE ICED TEA WITH A SLICE OF LEMON
ONE COFFEE, BLACK

Past the empty chapel
and hiding at the back
of the hospital
on ground level
ICU,
and a sign on the door says,
Family Only Please.
I walk through the door
where respirators breathe
into the mouths
of struggling patients.
The dance of green lines
shows the pulse of life,
while somber nurses
offer hushed comfort,
and doctors do what they can
when fate lies in divine hands.

His heart rate is 140. It's like he's running a marathon.

This can't be good.

All we can do is wait.

Dad used to run as a kid.

Your mother says resuscitate,
if and when the burdened heart stops
to give another life
although we don't now for how long,
but it's her say,
and she's the guardian
right or wrong,
but I cry to let him go.

…

She doesn't know what she's doing
except extending life of a tortured body
when his brain is already gone.
I don't understand her thoughts
and visions,
and she doesn't talk.
Heaven and other lives wait
but all she does is prolong.

…

It takes some people longer to let go
of the life they know. They cry eternity
can wait.

Log

Patient has been moved up to Room 830. Keep patient comfortable.

The nurse stands before me and speaks in a soft voice. "Your father's been weaned off the respirator and moved to eighth floor. The doctors have decided not to resuscitate; it's up to him."

I feel outside my body after another sleepless night. I feel as if I'm looking upon us. "So how is he this morning?"

"He's still hanging on."

"What could he be waiting for?"

A priest wears a purple stole as he leaves Dad's room.

A time of passage waits
Last Rites given,
and the priest leaves.
An angel waits by the door.

We'll keep your father comfortable,
that's what we promise to you,
and a turn of the pillow
might offer comfort,
we don't know.
The Christmas card you brought
we set on the dresser,
better late than never,
although he'll never notice
nor understand

Forced breaths speak many words
while Dad stares at the ceiling
as if facing his gods.
I notice his withered form
his feet barely push up the blanket.

I share few words without answer,
and pale under overhead light
he is already a ghost of himself.
I wonder to what part of him I speak
to what part of the brain, to what circuitry.

Forced breath says brain stem reason
life reduced to autonomic reflexes
while I wonder how long
for him
for me
when time has no mercy.

Mom lets me into her apartment from the cold. A kettle whistles as she heats water for her instant coffee.

I sit in the couch in the living room. Textbooks and spiral notebooks from my years at college and Dad's literature about machine tools clutter the room. When I wanted to throw away the books, she complained that they had spent a lot of money to send me to college.

I told her the knowledge was in my head.

I had agreed to let her keep them.

The room is full of memories, and they are in my head.

The television is turned on for sound. She brings me a Christmas cookie on a plate. She says that the people who drive her for errands left some.

"Mom, he's not doing well."

She doesn't say anything.

"I'll see him later." I excuse myself and go to my apartment, to read while the maintenance man fixes the sink.

I leave, and she gives me an awkward pat on the back. We don't hug; it's always been that way.

Snow covers the ground with silence.

Christmas lights strung up to form the skeleton of a tree on top of the hospital offer a soft glow. I walk with Mom without a word. It's not Christmas to me.

Sparrows on the sidewalk scatter. They fly to the parking lot and scavenge a bag of fast food.

Dad bought me a parakeet when I was in grade school. After seven years of fun, it died. We bought another.

He is my only dad. I bring a card he won't see.

Santa Claus walks around the lobby and gives children wrapped gifts.

A television screen shows black and white images of the empty hospital chapel as Mom and I walk into Dad's room. I figure the channel is to show masses and services for those who cannot attend. A candle burns.

The room feels too warm.

Dad stares at the ceiling. His breathing is forced; a bad sign I fear.

I stand next to the bed standing close to her.

An IV bag drips into a tube going to a vein on his arm. A nurse says, "It's a solution with sugar and vitamins to feed him."

"Maybe it will make him well," Mom says.

"It won't." I glance at her. "He's not going to make it," I say, using unblemished language, forcing myself to face the cold truth.

The nurse writes vitals on a clipboard. "His urine output is still good, but his body's shutting down."

Still I ask, "How soon?"

"It could be days or weeks."

The television still shows the chapel as we leave.

Dad occupies
the shell of a body
brainstem living
just enough to keep a heartbeat
and stir a labored breath.
He lies, neither asleep nor awake,
and I don't know if he hears
in body or in spirit, the few words
I say, of if he even sees my mom
standing next to me.
I tell her to wait in the hall
while I ponder time left,
a few days or a few weeks,
time so short, yet an eternity
unfinished business while spirit waits,
and I can only guess
what he wants from me.

"Mom, I must do this." I excuse myself and walk back into the room.

A past life comes to me. When I was a child, Dad took me shopping, and I spoke to him, only him, seeking the understanding only he could give. Father and son conversations were meant to be alone.

This I must do again.

Dad stares at the ceiling, knowing or not knowing. I tell myself he can hear. I must talk now; the spirits are near.

A bright light shines on him, just like the bright light before the Gates of Heaven I had seen in grade school Catechism.

Heaven or Reincarnation, it doesn't matter, just as long as he goes to a better place.

To him, and to him alone, I speak.
I know that it's right that alone I speak
to him and only him.

My voice fills the space between us,
answered by the silence of spirits
while surrounded by a calm
I cannot understand.

Dad, you may leave any time you want,
but don't leave or stay for me.
Leave when the time is right-
you have another life
somewhere beyond these lights.

Dad, leave your failing body behind-
You don't need it anymore.

Don't worry.
Mom has already chosen
a special place
in your childhood home,
and we will see you off
as you go to meet
your dad and mom.

I will take care of Mom.

An angel over the old entrance watches
as I leave with my mom while Christmas
         lights
above the hospital offer a soft glow
and season's greetings, but no words are
         spoken.
No plans are made- the family is broken.

While I drive alone, cold bites my soul,
and all I know is that I'm angry
at clouds and skies and stillness of winter.
I know he'll die, but in the spring
of my life, he was young, and I was
         younger.

The Christmas songs are gone
from the radio. I change channels. No song
is right, and lifeless skies are gray.

Why? I ask, where are the heavens
as they hide, and where are my gods?

I turn off the radio and listen to my thoughts,
and they are angry,
and the biting sky is angry
pressing upon me
in depths of winter.

I drop Mom at her apartment
with a promise to see her later.

Alone in my apartment
I take care of life's necessities
I play with a knickknack
on my stereo speaker
when I play a soft song
to ease the pain
I feel
I heat food
I eat
As a nurse says
I must
This food I cannot taste
must do-
I must go back.

The passage of Christmas
offers a new year,
Father Time and Baby New Year
changes calling
promises and resolutions
to be made and broken
time of passage,
but I wish better times for him
an incarnation
another life
where once again he is complete.

Snow covers ground
hides remnants of summer
as I walk around the park
where Dad and I used to go.

Bare trees in a wind
wave branches-
when they were full,
I drew them for him.

Bare branches point
their fingers at me.
I'm alone in the cold
a soliloquy.

Skies of gray
and biting cold
bear upon me-
angry, and I
don't know why.

I drive alone past parks where I played and past our old house.

A voice tells me to rush to the hospital. I wonder how reality interferes with the grief I am facing.

Gray skies, lit by city lights, look like snow. Feeling an adrenaline rush, I cry out, "No more."

While walking from the parking lot, a stone cross points upward from an entrance. The Christmas lights on top of the hospital are now turned off.

Christmas is over, and there's nothing.

Anger is better than feeling nothing.

A nurse at the station looks at me while I approach. "Your father has passed away."

"When?"

"Half an hour ago."

"I'm too late."

"The mortician is on his way, but you may visit him for a while."

The door to his room is closed. The room is on the top floor of the hospital, isolated from the rest of the hospital. That I figure is the way it was meant to be.

I open the door to go see him.

Bathed in bright light, Dad still looks as if he's staring at the ceiling, but his eyes are closed. I keep saying goodbye to him, as if his spirit is still in the room.

His spirit might be overhead, looking at us in the light, and the light might be the way to another day in another life, or to Heaven.

The television is still turned on to the closed circuit broadcast from the hospital chapel, still empty.

I wonder if his spirit is overhead, watching me.

I keep talking to him to recap memories. A nurse stands at the door and asks if I need anything. I ask for an iced tea with lemon. She gets it to me. Its taste with a touch of lemon is good.

I keep saying goodbye, as if one time is not enough for a lifetime passed.

It's been seven and a half years since he was placed in the Good Hope Home. I thought that it was enough to prepare me for this time, but it was not.

Dad is gone.

Log

Patient in Room 830 has died, and his wife has been called. We also have called the mortuary, and the mortician will be here soon.

The nurse lets me use a telephone in a private space to call my aunt, my mom's sister. It's up to me to tell her. "He didn't make it," I say.

I close my eyes and am intrigued by the image of a man swimming across a lake. Blue waters reflect sunlight.

The dark skies are clear when I drive to Mom's apartment. I find the cold air refreshing.

It's late, but I knock on her door. She's still up, and she leads me into the living room, barely lit.

"Dad didn't make it."

"I know; the hospital called."

"He was a good man." I am unsure of what to say.

"Do you want something to eat?"

"Would you give me a cookie?" I am tired, and figure chocolate and sugar will keep me going. "This is strange," I say.

She nods. "Someone from the nursing home called and asked that someone gets his clothes." She pauses. "You might be able to use something."

"I'll get it tonight."

Wearing a sad expression, she stands at the front door as I leave.

She understands.

A cold breeze beckons. The air is clear, a moment of clarity.

night dreams
night whispers
light shimmers
dark skies clear
spirits call
clear skies dark
shimmers light
whispers night
dreams night

A light illuminates the entrance of Building 2 at the Good Hope Home. Inside, the hallways are silent, silent enough to allow words of my father to echo in my mind.

Two nurses stand at the station and converse. One looks at me. She knows. I tell her that I am coming to get Dad's clothes.

"They're already boxed up."

I nod at her. Words fail me.

The bed inside his room is untouched. Two boxes are inside a closet.

I look through the clothing, and in one box is the red sweatshirt with the words *IOWA STATE UNIVERSITY* in gold. I try it on, and it fits.

I keep it on and walk to the nurse's station. "Donate the rest."

The nurses agree.

"How's Becky?" I ask.

"She stopped by and said she's doing well."

A light shines on a portrait of an angel hanging on the wall.

Three days later, sun breaks through the clouds. Frigid air grips me as I step out my apartment building. Although weary, I take the usual early morning run. Packed snow covers the bike path, but instinct tells me to continue. Blood pulses through me, and I know there is more life inside me. A nearby creek flows under a shelf of ice. I want to stop and look at it, but my Dad's burial is soon.

Just one more month and he'd be seventy-eight. Back home I look at a clock on the wall and figure everything has its time. I wonder why he couldn't have lived until his birthday, in just a week, but figure the passage spared him and my family more suffering.

I grab a sweet roll and down it, to have something to get me through the day.

Adrenaline flows through me as I pick up Mom and go to the funeral home. When I get there, the people who drive Mom on her errands are already there. They agreed to drive us to the burial. My car needs repair before I can take it on the highway.

They stay inside their car as Mom and I take one more look at Dad before the coffin is shut.

A light inside a room at the funeral home shines on him. Age has descended upon him. His hair, now gray, is swept back to cover the crown on the back of his head. His hands are clasped.

He wears a stoic expression, as if he has accepted what has come.

"They did a good job with him," Mom says.

"They did." I sigh.

I close my eyes to envision him younger once more.

We follow the hearse down an Interstate highway to his old hometown. Cars pass, drivers on the way to their separate lives. The ride is smooth, and I take comfort in scenery I've seen many times.

The sun pokes through a wall of gray clouds as the hearse leads us to his hometown. Silhouetted trees in a grove reach for the sky.

A biting cold breeze greets us as we stand at the grave. Flowers Mom chose cover the coffin. She had made arrangements long before he was ill, and she had reserved a spot for her next to him.

The driver and his wife join us. In a hushed voice, she says, "I never met your dad, but from all I heard, I feel that I knew him, too."

"He was a great man," I say.

"I'm sure he was."

A priest from a nearby parish offers prayers for comfort. I wonder what I feel. Although my religion is undefined, I pray to spirits in the breeze, winter's soft song.

I turn to Mom. "He doesn't have to worry about anything. His job is done."

Dad never wanted to retire, but his machinery tool sales business failed during the farm crisis. He said that people in his hometown, a railroad town, died soon after retiring.

FARMERS FACING FINANCIAL TROUBLE = NO TRACTOR AND COMBINE SALES = NO SALES OF MACHINE TOOL SALES

Dad worked his first job at a bulldozer factory near his childhood home. He said that he worked two machine tools at one time for a quarter-per-hour raise.

"He's back home," I say to her.

"He's near his mother and father," she says.

Alzheimer's
What brought it on?
Was it Dad's losses
that maybe
he couldn't face,
or was it something else?
The first day
at the Good Hope Home
he saw a footrest
and tried to sell
me a machine tool.
I called it a machine tool
for his sake.

I'm left with one thought:
I'm my father's son.

Driven to closeness
after Dad's passage,
Mom and I ride in the back seat
on a hushed winter day.

Cleared roads offer safe travel,
and snow on the ground
silences the journey back
left for two together.

I wonder what to say
as I reclaim my mother
and shared memories
as we sit side by side,
two people
looking at one loss
in two different ways
father from son
husband from wife

when tree limbs stripped bare
reach like angel wings
toward the sun
as if in prayer.

After we get back Mom and I stand alone in the parking lot of the mortuary while her driver waits. The sun to the west wears a halo of orange. Shadows are cast as I wonder what happened to the day.

It seems just like yesterday when I was playing on a summer day in my parents' backyard. I think about how my father kept a sense of youth until after he was placed in the nursing home. I think about how life complicates itself and the natural order.

"It's going to snow," I say.

"I suppose it is."

"Dad's going to miss this one."

"It will be warmer for him."

"I'll see you tomorrow." We give each other an awkward hug, and I think about how I am her son.

Back in my apartment, I close my eyes and see Dad running a mile all out in quiet streets of his hometown.

I had started with a mile, and as he watched, I learned to do the marathon. Life is a marathon.

In the soft darkness of my apartment I get ready for bed. I take a moment to pull a shade and look at a light beyond the parking lot.

I let out a weary laugh and look through a veil of glistening snow and look deep into darkness for the place where stars hide.

Alone I wake in the middle of the night and listen to some kind of sound. I call it a vibration. There is no other word to describe it.

I close my eyes and lie on my back as waking life flows out of me. There is a face.

A familiar voice comes to me:

> Son, what happened wasn't so bad. It was kind of like
> learning to swim. Someone throws you into a quarry,
> and it's sink or rise to the top. Someone threw me into
> the quarry when I was a kid. I did okay.

> I wanted to get back to you as soon as I could, so you
> don't worry. I'm just here floating on my back, and the
> sky is blue.

ABOUT THE AUTHOR

Mike Bayles, a life-long Midwest resident, has lived in mid-sized cities, small towns, and rural areas in Iowa, Minnesota, and Illinois. While spending summers at a cottage on a lake in Minnesota, he found a deep appreciation for nature. He enjoyed family life as an only child, but also enjoyed visiting aunts, uncles, and cousins on their farms. He attended Iowa State University and The University of Northern Iowa, where he received a B.A. in Sociology